At the Side of
RUTH

By the same author:

At the Side of David
A Multiple-Ending Bible Adventure

At the Side of Esther
A Multiple-Ending Bible Adventure

At the Side of Moses
A Multiple-Ending Bible Adventure

At the Side of
RUTH

A Multiple-Ending
Bible Adventure

Written by
Eric Pakulak

Illustrated by
Danny Bulanadi

Pauline
BOOKS & MEDIA
BOSTON

Library of Congress Cataloging-in-Publication Data

Pakulak, Eric.
   At the side of Ruth : a multiple-ending Bible adventure /
written by Eric Pakulak ; illustrated by Danny Bulanadi.
        p. cm.
Summary: As the fictional friend of Ruth, the reader makes
decisions about whether to leave her homeland and go with
Naomi and Ruth or to stay in Moab, with different plot
developments depending on the choices.
   ISBN 0-8198-0771-0 (pbk.)
   1.   Ruth (Biblical figure)—Juvenile fiction. 2.   Plot-your-
own stories. [1. Ruth (Biblical figure)—Fiction. 2.   Plot-
your-own stories.] I. Bulanadi, Danny, ill. II. Title.
   PZ7.P174 Av 2000
   [Fic]—dc21

                                    00-010194

Printed and published in the U.S.A. by Pauline Books & Media,
50 Saint Pauls Avenue, Boston MA 02130-3491.

www.pauline.org

Pauline Books & Media is the publishing house of the
Daughters of St. Paul, an international congregation of women
religious serving the Church with the communications media.

1 2 3 4 5 6   05 04 03 02 01

*For Mom and Dad,
whose love and support
mean more than
words can express*

About This Book...

At the Side of Ruth is based on the Bible's story of Ruth, a young woman who left her family, her country, and all that she had in a special act of love that was rewarded by God.

As you read, you will relive the story as Ruth's *imaginary* friend. You'll even have your own choices to make.

The author and the publisher hope that interacting with this Bible story will help you to think about the values that made Ruth, who was not herself a Jew, one of the great women in Jewish history.

T he rays of the morning sun are already breaking through the trees as you take your daily walk through the hillside fields of Moab, your homeland. You might be imagining it, but you think you hear sobbing close by. Behind a cluster of shrubbery, you suddenly come upon your friend Ruth and her sister-in-law Orpah. They're sitting on a boulder, quietly weeping.

"What's the matter?" you gently ask.

You find it hard to imagine what further sadness could visit the young women. Just last month both of their husbands, Mahlon and Chilion, died.

"It's Naomi," Ruth manages to say between sobs. "Word has come that the famine in Israel is over, and now she wants to leave us and return to Bethlehem."

Naomi is the mother-in-law of Ruth and Orpah. You know that she's suffered much in her life. Ten years ago she came to Moab, fleeing the famine with her husband Elimelech and their two sons Mahlon and Chilion. Elimelech died almost as soon as they arrived. And now her sons are gone.

You feel sorry for Naomi. She's always been very kind to you and has helped you many times with wise advice. You can understand why she wants to return to Israel. It's the land of her birth and the land of the one true God of whom she has spoken so often. Here in Moab the people don't worship this God. They adore the sun and the stars instead.

As you try to comfort Ruth and Orpah, Naomi herself comes up the trail. "I'm leaving for Israel now," she says, kissing her daughters-in-law good-bye. "Go back to your mothers, and may God grant you happiness with new husbands here in your homeland."

As Naomi walks away, Ruth and Orpah follow her. "We'll return with you to the land of your people," they say, still weeping.

"No, no," replies Naomi. "What good am I to you? I'm too old to marry again, and even if I had a husband and were to bear two sons tonight, would you just sit and wait for them to be old enough to marry? No, you must stay here with your people."

"Perhaps you're right," Orpah says sadly as she hugs Naomi. "This is my land, my people. We have our own religion. I should stay here."

As Orpah leaves, Naomi turns to Ruth. "Look, your sister-in-law has gone back to her people and her gods. Return with her," she pleads.

"Please don't make me leave you!" Ruth begs. "Wherever you go I will go; wherever you stay I will stay. Your people will be my people, and your God will be my God. Only death will separate us."

You feel torn. You love Naomi, and Ruth has been your best friend for many years. You could ask to go with them, but it will be difficult to leave your homeland and change your religion.

If you catch up with Orpah and stay with her in Moab, turn to page 11.

If you go with Ruth and Naomi to Israel, turn to page 12.

With tears filling your eyes, you embrace Ruth and Naomi and wish them well on their journey to Bethlehem.

"Farewell my friend," sobs Ruth.

"May the Lord be with you," whispers Naomi, "always."

You turn and hurry to catch up with Orpah. After a few minutes you find her resting in the shade of a grove of trees. Her tears have dried, and she seems happy to see you.

"I thought you'd go with them," she says, "but it's probably best to remain in our country and follow our own religion."

"Yes," you agree, still thinking of Ruth.

The two of you return to your village. You soon notice that things seem empty and quiet without Ruth and Naomi. You think of setting out by yourself to find them, but the journey might be too difficult to make alone. Besides, you'll probably get over your loneliness in a few weeks.

If you set out alone to try to find Ruth and Naomi, turn to page 16.

If you stay in Moab, turn to page 20.

Though it's certainly a big step to move to a country you've never even visited before, you feel happy with your decision.

"I can't leave you," you say. "I must come too."

The three of you share a warm embrace, then immediately go to prepare for the journey. You're nervous but also very excited at the thought of the adventure that lies ahead of you. After packing your favorite donkey, you meet up with Ruth and Naomi and set off.

It's a warm, sunny day, perfect for traveling. By midday you find yourself before the River Jordan, the border between Moab and Israel. The river's current is swift. You glance at Ruth. You can tell by her expression that she shares your hesitation about crossing the river. Sensing this, Naomi takes you both by the hand, and the three of you venture into the cold water together. About halfway across, with the rapids up to your waists, you begin to get frightened. Naomi stops. "Now think of God," she says calmly. "Feel him here with us. Receive strength from him."

Naomi squeezes your hand, and you have a strong sense that her God is also watching over you. It's a wonderful feeling! Together you push onward with determination and quickly reach the shore. A few hours later, you set up camp for the night.

You sleep very well on your first night in Israel. The presence of your friends and the thought of their God bring you comfort and a sense of security.

Naomi, anxious to reach Bethlehem, wakes you and Ruth early the next morning. You eagerly continue on the road beneath a brilliant sun.

After a long day of travel, the hillside city finally appears on a ridge up ahead. As you approach Bethlehem's gates, you see houses of sunburnt brick rising beyond the city wall. Once you've entered the gate, people begin to recognize Naomi. In no time a small group has gathered around the three of you.

"Naomi, is it *really* you?" asks one of the women.

"Yes," she says with tears in her eyes. "But do not call me Naomi. Call me Mara, for the Lord has dealt bitterly with me."

Realizing that the name Mara means "sad" or "bitter," you also feel tears filling your eyes.

"I went out full and the Lord has brought me home empty," Naomi continues. "How can you call me Naomi, which means delight, when the Lord has treated me so?"

As Naomi continues to speak with her friends, Ruth takes you aside. "I've heard it's very difficult for a poor widow to live in this city," she quietly tells you. "I want to help Naomi by going to glean grain in the fields."

You've heard of the law that allows those who are too poor to have a field of their own to go into the fields of others and glean, or gather the grain left behind by the reapers. You don't consider yourself a beggar, and you're not sure you're ready to resort to this backbreaking work among the poorest of the poor when you haven't even explored other job possibilities in the city. But ...you *do* want to help Naomi. Maybe Ruth's idea is a good one.

If you decide not to go glean grain in the fields with Ruth, turn to page 22.

If you go with Ruth to the fields, turn to page 23.

You explain to Orpah and your other friends that your heart is with Ruth, pack up your favorite donkey, and leave as quickly as you can. The journey to Bethlehem is over fifty miles through country you've never seen before, but you're determined to catch up with your best friend.

The sun blazes bright in the clear sky, providing excellent weather for travel, and you're able to make good time. By midafternoon you hear the rush of water. Minutes later you round a bend and find yourself facing the mighty river Jordan, the border of Israel, its fast-moving current glistening in the sunlight.

The trail leads down to a small bank before some shallow but swift rapids. This is the place where, you've heard, those with faith in God can ford the river safely. You remember the true God Naomi has so often spoken of, but the river does look a bit dangerous.

As you stand on the bank deciding whether or not to attempt a crossing, a cloud moves in front of the sun, slowly darkening the sky. In the religion of Moab this is a bad omen. Perhaps it would be wiser to go upstream in search of a bridge or a ferryboat.

If you go upstream in search of a safer crossing, turn to page 18.

If you try to ford the river through the rapids, turn to page 19.

Deciding not to brave the rapids, you head upstream. The clouds continue to hide the sun, and soon a light rain is falling. The trail along the riverbank is beginning to fade as the underbrush gets thicker. Every time you fight your way through a thicket you expect to see a bridge or a friendly ferryman, but all you find is the empty river.

As you press on, the sky gets darker and the rain heavier. The ground has turned to mud, and your donkey can hardly move. *I should call upon Naomi's God,* you think. *She says he is very good and merciful…. God of Naomi's people, please help me!* you pray in your heart.

After this prayer you feel calmer and more courageous. You also realize that maybe it *is* too dangerous to try to reach Israel on your own. You slowly make your way back to Moab. But for the rest of your life you regret not having gone with Naomi and Ruth.

The End

You close your eyes, take a deep breath, and head out into the river. Your entire body shivers with the first chill of the water. Slowly but surely you move farther out. Soon the water is up to your waist. The current is even stronger than you thought, and you lose your balance, almost falling in!

Now, shaking from nerves more than cold, you see that you're not even halfway across. You consider turning back. Instead, you stop, close your eyes, and think of Naomi's one true God. Whispering a prayer, you ask him for the strength to make it to the other side. You gradually feel a warmth in your heart, and a sense of calm spreads over your whole body. Opening your eyes and releasing a deep breath, you continue across with more confidence in your step. Before you even realize it, you're standing in Israel, feeling refreshed and revived.

You continue on your journey, and after only an hour you come upon the camp of Ruth and Naomi. They welcome you with open arms, give you a hot meal, and tell you how happy they are that you will be going with them to Bethlehem.

Turn to page 13.

Although life will never be the same without your best friend Ruth, you've decided that you belong in Moab. After a few weeks you've settled into a new routine, working extra hard in the fields as you try to ignore your loneliness.

As time goes by, you become friendlier with Orpah, but the two of you never talk the way you and Ruth used to. You really miss your best friend and feel lost and empty without her. You're tempted to go to Bethlehem and try to find her, but you realize that this would be useless.

After a while you decide to try to fill the emptiness in your life by becoming more involved in religion. Although you're still curious about Naomi's one true God, your people worship nature. One day, as the elders are preparing for a fire ceremony to honor the Moabite god Chemosh, they send you out to climb trees and gather branches. Though you're not a very good climber, you're anxious to please the elders.

After a short hike, you reach the woods. Looking up, you don't ever remember trees being so tall! You take a deep breath to calm your nerves and begin climbing. You climb carefully and steadily, breaking off and dropping branches to pick up later. Everything is fine until you make the mistake of looking down. That's when your heart starts pounding and your breathing quickens. You shut your eyes, but you can't help thinking of the distance to the ground below you. Finally you begin your slow climb down. Your body is tense and stiff. At a critical point, your foot misses a branch. As you plunge toward the forest floor you have only one thought—Naomi's God! "Help me!" you cry to him.

You come crashing through some entangled branches that help to break your fall. Bruised and frightened, you lie on the ground. *Even though I don't yet know you, I thank you!* you pray to the God of the Israelites.

The End

"I want to help Naomi too, Ruth, but there must be a better way. If I look around Bethlehem," you tell her, "I might find some more dignified work."

"There's no dignity lost in doing whatever I can to help my mother-in-law," Ruth quietly replies. "But I wish you luck in finding work. Be careful now, and promise to meet me at the end of the day."

"I promise," you smile back.

Though you're a little nervous about being on your own in a strange land, you set off. The city is a confusing swirl of activity, and you realize that finding work will not be as easy as you thought. Eventually you come across an open-air market. Here foreign merchants are selling many different types of wares. Stopping at a booth, you ask the merchant whether he's looking for help. He rubs his chin in thought, then beckons you to follow him. He leads you into a large tent, where he begins speaking with another merchant in a strange language. You get an uneasy feeling and turn to leave, but the men block your way. As others in the tent surround you, you realize in panic that these are slave dealers! Now you'll never keep your promise to Ruth...

The End

"I want to help Naomi," you tell Ruth. "I'll come to glean with you."

The next day Ruth awakens you as the first rays of the springtime sun are creeping over the hills. She smiles as you yawn and sleepily rub your eyes. "It's best that we get an early start," she says cheerfully. You nod and soon the two of you are on your way to the fields.

As you reach the outskirts of Bethlehem, you see the reapers gathering in preparation for the long day ahead. Although there are many different fields before you, Ruth seems drawn to a large one just to the right of the road, and you approach the workers waiting there.

"Please let me glean and gather after your reapers," Ruth says quietly.

The men agree, and in a few minutes you find yourself beside Ruth scooping up the grain left behind by the reapers. Though there isn't much grain left after the reaping, the law states that the reapers must leave some on the ground for the poor to collect. You're amazed at how fast Ruth is able to work. It's not easy to keep up with her. Little by little more poor people from the city arrive, and this seems to make Ruth work even faster.

By late morning your back is aching from the constant bending, and your arms are sore from carrying the grain. What's worse, your head is throbbing from the merciless heat of the sun. Off to the side of the field you see a large tree casting an inviting shadow. *It would feel so good to rest in the shade for a few minutes,* you think. *But what if I fall behind and lose Ruth?*

If you go off to rest under the tree, turn to page 25.

If you continue working, turn to page 27.

You tap Ruth on the shoulder and tell her that you want to stop for a short rest. Though she looks disappointed, she tells you to do what you feel you must, and turns back to her work.

You slow down and let all the reapers and other gleaners pass, then slip off to the shade of the tree. The coolness immediately eases the throbbing of your head and the soreness of your muscles. Your eyelids are heavy. Before you realize what's happening, you fall into a deep sleep.

The next thing you know, one of the reapers is shaking you by the shoulders. As your eyes adjust to the bright light, you see several more men standing above you.

"The field is a place to work," says one sternly, "not to sleep. Please leave now and do not return."

You have no choice. As you get up, you scan the field for Ruth, but she's nowhere in sight. You return to Bethlehem to look for Naomi, but she's not where you left her. Thinking that she must be visiting friends in the city, you set out to find her. You jostle your way through the narrow, crowded streets. But there's no sign of Naomi anywhere. You begin to feel strangely dizzy in the midday heat. All the shops and unfamiliar faces seem to blur together as you realize that you're lost! You try to find your way back, but it's hopeless. After hours of wandering in the heat, your hands tremble, and your face burns with a fever. By nightfall you find yourself slumping against a wall in a side alley, slowly losing consciousness...

You awaken to a cool morning breeze flapping the doors of the white tent in which you're lying, covered in soft linen. A woman sitting nearby notices that you've opened your eyes. She comes over to you. "My husband found you on the street," she says in a sympathetic voice. "You've been very sick for three days." The woman goes on to explain that she and her family are traveling merchants, and even though they were on their way out of Bethlehem, they felt they must help you, and so took you with them. "We need a servant," the woman adds gently. "When you're well, you would be welcome to stay with us."

Since you have no way to return to Bethlehem now, and since these kind strangers have saved your life, you decide to remain with them. Your life from then on is a very interesting one as you travel from one land to another. But it's also a very lonely life, because you never find anyone to replace your best friend. You spend many nights gazing back toward Bethlehem, wondering whatever happened to Ruth...

The End

A quick rest is tempting, but Ruth's example inspires you to push on. You know that she must be just as hot and tired as you are. But she never complains.

After a few more hours of work, you stand up to stretch your back and notice a man approaching. He's very tall and handsome, with wavy black hair, heavy eyebrows, and a flowing beard. You realize that he must be someone important, because his robe is decorated with beautiful embroidery, and several servants are following him. He stops at the edge of the field where you're working and raises his arms.

"The Lord be with you," he says in a deep, resounding voice. You follow the lead of the reapers and the other workers and turn toward him.

"The Lord bless you," answer all the workers.

Though Ruth immediately turns back to her work, your gaze lingers on the man. You notice him gesturing toward Ruth as he speaks to the servant who is overseeing the harvesting. When they finish speaking, the wealthy-looking man smiles and approaches Ruth.

"Don't go to glean in another man's field, my daughter," he says kindly. "Stay here with my women servants. If you are thirsty, go drink from the water that my young men have drawn. I have told them not to harm you."

You hear Ruth gasp. She's as surprised as you are at the field owner's unexpected words. She drops the grain in her hands and bows down before him.

"Why do you treat me with such kindness," she asks, looking up at the man, "when I am a stranger in this land?"

"I have heard of the kindness with which you've treated your mother-in-law Naomi," he replies, "and of the courage you've shown in leaving your native land to come here. May the Lord, the God of Israel, reward you."

With tears in her eyes, Ruth thanks the man for his generosity. He smiles and invites her to come eat with him and his gleaners at mealtime.

As the man walks away, you have mixed feelings. He *seems* genuinely kind, and you and Ruth can certainly use some help. But it *is* a bit unusual for a complete stranger to make such generous offers. You wonder if you should try to find out more about him…

If you leave Ruth to try to find out more about this man, turn to page 30.

If you continue working with Ruth and go to eat at the man's table, turn to page 34.

"I'm a little suspicious of this stranger," you tell Ruth. "Why is he being so good to you? It might be wise to find out more about him before accepting his invitation to a meal."

Ruth closes her eyes, takes a deep breath, and thinks for a moment. "Do as you wish, my friend," she says. "But I truly felt the Lord when he spoke, and I have faith that he is a good man."

Although Ruth's words make you feel better, you would still rather find out more about the kind stranger. You say good-bye to Ruth, telling her that you hope to return soon.

Hurrying from the field, you take the main road to Bethlehem. It's a beautiful day, and the route is crowded with travelers whose robes flutter in the light afternoon breeze. You approach an older couple, a man and woman leading a cart that is apparently filled with all of their possessions.

"Excuse me," you ask, "do you know the owner of those fields behind us?"

"No, young one," the man replies. "We haven't been here long, and now we're on our way back to Moab."

"I'm from Moab, too!" you excitedly reply.

Before you know it, you find yourself reminiscing about your homeland. The woman tells you how much they miss Moab and explains that they are returning there because they couldn't get used to this land and its people's religion. She talks about the religion practiced in Moab, where people worship the natural elements like fire and water. "Worshipping the earth makes more sense to me than worshipping the God of the Israelites who can't be seen," she tells you.

Her husband nods. "You're welcome to travel back to Moab with us if you'd like," he adds.

As you think about this offer, you realize that you have a difficult decision to make. You wonder whether you wouldn't be happier back in Moab, even though it would mean leaving your best friend. At the same time, you *are* curious about this one true God of the Israelites, especially after what happened with the mysterious owner of the fields.

If you accept the offer to return to Moab, turn to page 32.

If you stay and continue trying to learn more about the owner of the fields, turn to page 33.

"Thank you," you tell the couple. "It's very hard for me to leave my friend Ruth, but I really do miss Moab. I'd like to come with you."

The husband and wife seem happy to have a traveling companion, and your lively conversation makes the hours slip by quickly. You learn that they know Ruth's sister-in-law Orpah, and after a safe and peaceful journey they take you to Orpah's home.

Turn to page 20.

You thank the couple for their generous offer, but explain that you can't leave your best friend Ruth. Wishing them a safe journey, you watch them slowly disappear into the crowd.

Remembering what you set out to do, you turn to the next group of people, three women carrying parcels of threshed grain. Again you ask about the man who spoke to you in his field.

"Oh!" exclaims one of the women. "Everyone knows him. He's Boaz, a very good and generous man."

"Yes," adds another, "a true servant of the Lord."

"It is said," says the third woman, "that those who have faith can feel the strength of the Lord when Boaz speaks."

You thank them and head back to find Ruth. You're hot and tired when you finally catch up with her in the field. Luckily for you, just as you arrive a servant approaches and announces that it's mealtime.

Turn to page 35.

Once the man has left, you pause for a moment before stooping to gather more grain. You see that Ruth is already hard at work, a peaceful smile on her face. You're still thinking about the unexpected encounter with the kind stranger. "Ruth, why are you so ready to trust this man?" you ask.

"I felt something when he spoke," Ruth answers. "I can't explain it, but I felt that God was with him. I have faith that he's a good man."

You smile and, feeling a burst of energy, go back to your work. It's very hot out and there's no shade nearby. Finally, just as you're starting to feel as if you can't go on, one of the field owner's servants announces that it's mealtime.

Go to the next page.

Following the other workers to the edge of the owner's property, you come upon a large table full of food and vessels of water. You see the field owner sitting at the head of the table, surrounded by servants. Following Ruth's lead, you sit with the other workers at the far end of the table. When the man sees that Ruth is at the table, he immediately gets up and walks toward you with a plate.

"My name is Boaz," he says. "Welcome to my table. Here's some of my best parched corn. Please take as much as you like."

Boaz tells you how delicious the corn is when you dip it in one of the bowls of vinegar set out on the table. You try it, and discover that it is very good. You and Ruth are both very hungry and you eat with pleasure. Before she's finished the food on her plate, however, and before any of the other workers have finished, Ruth gets up.

"I can eat later," she whispers to you. "Right now I want to work so that I can bring as much grain as possible back to Naomi."

With that, she walks off toward the field. Boaz notices this, and a smile comes over his face. He motions to his reapers to gather around him. "Let her work among you for as long as she wants," he instructs them, "and purposely drop some handfuls of grain for her."

The workers nod in agreement and go to finish their meal. Boaz and his servants then get up to leave. In a few minutes, the reapers are on their way back to the field. Standing up to follow, you realize that you're very tired and sore, and still a little hungry. There is plenty of food left on the table. Maybe no one would mind if you rested a bit longer and had something more to eat. But Ruth is already hard at work in spite of her own hunger and soreness, and you *did* come to the field in order to help Naomi.

If you stay behind to rest and eat more, turn to page 38.

If you go back out to work with Ruth, turn to page 39.

You stand quietly to one side as the workers walk off. No one notices you, and soon you have the whole table to yourself. You sit back down and eat some more parched corn. Now that you're no longer hungry, you begin to feel drowsy. You decide that it would be best to lie down for a while before going back to work. You find a shady tree some distance from the field and settle under it for a quick rest...

Kaboom!! A deafening crash makes you jump to your feet. It's dark now, so dark that you can see nothing around you. You must have slept for hours! A steady rain beats down on your face as you strain to see. Suddenly a bright flash lights the sky, and you realize that you're caught in a thunderstorm. All the field workers are gone. You're completely alone. By now Ruth is back in Bethlehem, but it would be impossible for you to find your way there in this storm. Trying not to panic, you cling to the tree for shelter. Unfortunately, that's the worst thing you could do under the circumstances. The sky again flashes, the tree shudders in your arms, and the last thing you see is a shower of sparks from above.

The End

Even though your muscles ache with every step, you follow the workers back to the field and take your place beside Ruth. You see how the workers have obeyed Boaz. You and Ruth are allowed to glean closer to the harvesters, where there is more grain. You also notice the men purposely dropping large handfuls of grain for you to gather. Seeing the smile on Ruth's face as she wipes the perspiration from her brow renews your energy, and you're almost able to keep up with her.

You're so intent on collecting as much grain as possible that time passes quickly. Before you know it, the sun has dissolved into a beautiful reddish glow on the horizon. As it begins to get dark, one of the workers announces that it's time to stop for the day. The men bring out containers, and you and Ruth beat out the grains of barley you've gathered. Ruth is able to fill a large container, called an ephah, all the way to the top. While you don't have quite as much as Ruth, you're still proud to be able to fill a smaller container. Carrying your precious grain, the two of you walk back to Naomi's house. Her eyes open wide, then fill with tears when she sees how much barley you've brought. Ruth has also brought some parched corn she saved from the meal at Boaz's table.

"Praise the Lord!" Naomi exclaims with emotion as she gives Ruth a big hug. "Where did you glean today? Bless him who took notice of you and showed you so much kindness."

"The man in whose field I gleaned today is very kind," says Ruth. "His name is Boaz."

"Blessed be the Lord!" cries Naomi. "Boaz is one of our kinsmen. He was related to my husband."

"He allowed me to glean close to his workers," explains Ruth. "He even told me that I may gather in his field until the end of harvest."

"This is good, my daughter," replies Naomi. "Go out again and stay close to his workers, and do not glean in any other field."

Ruth tells Naomi that she'll be up early the next morning to go back to work in Boaz's field. Your aching body protests at the thought of another long day of backbreaking work. You wonder if it might be best to take a day to let your sore muscles rest. But you also remember Ruth's desire to help Naomi.

If you decide not to go to the fields tomorrow, turn to page 41.

If you go back to work with Ruth, turn to page 43.

You tell Ruth and Naomi how tired and sore you are. "I really do need to rest," you explain.

Naomi begins to speak of sacrifice at the time of harvest, but Ruth stops her and puts her hand on your shoulder. "Do whatever you feel is best," she says with a gentle smile.

The next morning you hear Ruth leaving for the fields at dawn, but you quickly go back to sleep. When you finally get up, it's midmorning and Naomi has already left for the day. A full night's sleep has given you new energy and you feel much better.

You decide to go out and explore Bethlehem. The marketplace is noisy and crowded. Wanting to escape this, you head for the city wall. You find your way out of one of the side gates. As you look up to admire the cloudless sky, you suddenly trip and fall on a rock that's been dislodged from the base of the wall. Pulling yourself to a sitting position, you feel a throbbing sensation in your left ankle. Now it's beginning to swell. *I must get back to Naomi's,* you think in panic. Leaning against the wall for support, and dragging your left foot behind you, you struggle through the closest gate. Once inside the city wall you sit by the marketplace, hoping to find someone to help you. After what seems like hours, one of the overseers of Boaz's field comes by with his wife. Fortunately, he recognizes you and offers to take you back to Naomi's home in his wagon.

Your ankle is seriously sprained, and it will be several days before you can join Ruth in the fields again. You feel really bad about having to stay at home and do nothing while Ruth is working extra hard to provide for both you and Naomi...

The End

Naomi's joyful reaction to the barley Ruth and you brought home is enough to help you overcome your soreness, and the next morning you're up at dawn with Ruth and on your way to work. At the field Boaz's workers give you a friendly welcome and again allow you to glean close to them. At first it's very difficult. Your whole body aches each time you bend down to pick up the grains left behind by the men. Surprisingly though, you find that the more work you do the better you feel, especially as the morning sun rises higher and warms your back.

Mealtime comes soon enough. Again you're invited to eat at the table with Boaz and his workers. Today the table is set by the road, and after the meal you decide to take a short walk before returning to the fields. "Come with me, Ruth," you call. "Just for a few minutes."

"Thank you," Ruth smiles. "But I think I'll sit here a bit longer."

You walk up the road enjoying a refreshing breeze. As you're about to turn back, you notice two young men sitting on a bench by the roadside. It's actually their robes that catch your attention. These robes are even more elaborate than those worn by Boaz, and they are richly embroidered in gold.

The men motion to you to come over. "Hello, friend," one of them says. "Are you coming from the fields?"

"Yes," you reply. "I'm poor, so I glean behind the workers."

"You need not be poor," they say. "Look at us, at our beautiful robes."

"I was just admiring them," you admit.

The young men explain that their father has given them land to teach them the proper way to run a business. "Do you want to live in poverty for the rest of your life?" one asks.

"No," you answer with embarrassment.

"Then come and work for us," one of the brothers says.

If you go with the men, turn to page 46.

If you refuse their invitation and go back to work in Boaz's field, turn to page 50.

You accept their offer, and you follow them back to their property. As you're walking along, you think about the happiness you'll bring to Ruth and Naomi when you return with your unexpected pay.

The brothers' field is apparently farther than you thought, since you've been walking for more than half an hour. Bethlehem is looking more and more distant.

"Are we almost there?" you ask.

"It's just around this corner," one of the men answers. "By the way, where did you work before?"

"In the field of Boaz," you reply.

The men laugh. "Boaz?" one says. "He's an old fool! He's so generous to the poor that he throws away his own profits."

Hearing this makes you feel a little uncomfortable, since you've found Boaz to be a good man. You begin to have second thoughts, especially because it's already getting late and Ruth might be worried. But what if the men pay you very well? That will be worth causing Ruth a little worry.

If you turn back and go try to find Ruth, turn to page 47.

If you stay with the men, turn to page 49.

"Thank you," you say, "but Boaz is a good man and I think I'll return to work in his field with my friend Ruth."

"No you won't," one of the men says, as both step closer to you. You begin to back away.

"You've already agreed to work for us," the older of the two continues angrily. "Under the law, that makes you our slave!"

Suddenly both brothers reach out to grasp your arms. You turn to run, but one catches hold of the end of your robe. Summoning all your strength, you break free and run. One brother begins to chase you down the road. You know you can't outrun him, so you jump into a clump of bushes. After a tumble down a hill, you end up hiding behind a large tree. You see the brothers searching through the bushes, then shaking their heads and walking away.

After some time, you cautiously steal back to the road. You're a little scratched, but otherwise fine. There's no sign of the men, but you still run much of the way back to Bethlehem. By the time you reach the main road to the city, the sun is already beginning to set. You decide to go straight to Naomi's house rather than try to return to the field. You're happy to find Naomi at home when you arrive. She listens breathlessly to your story, then hugs you tightly.

When Ruth comes home, she's very relieved to see you. "I appreciate your good intentions, but it's better to be wealthy in friendship than in gold," she tells you.

You have to agree that she's right.

Turn to page 51.

You decide to overlook their rude comments about Boaz, thinking of the money you might earn. You follow the men down the narrow road that leads to their property. A group of workers comes into view. As you reach them, you see that these workers look nothing like those employed by Boaz. Unlike the fresh white robes of Boaz's workers, their robes are stained with dirt and grime. Their sunken eyes have a strange, faraway look. You also notice that there are no gleaners following behind the workers. You feel a shiver run down your spine and slow your step, but the men take you by the arms and lead you into the field. You put aside all thoughts of escaping when you see three guards standing nearby, swords in hand.

"When you agreed to come with us," one of the men says, "you became our slave by law. Now get to work!"

Your life as a slave becomes a dull routine. You work hard from dawn to dusk with little food or time for rest. After the harvest, you're sold and taken far from Bethlehem to work on the building of a new temple. Though you eventually accept your new life, you always regret having been blinded by greed. You know now that no amount of money could ever be worth losing your freedom…and your best friend.

The End

You thank the men for their offer, but tell them that you're happy gleaning in the field with your friend Ruth. You hurry back and finish another day of good, hard work. Later you tell Ruth and Naomi about your encounter with the men.

"They may have been trying to lure foreigners into slavery," Naomi tells you. "It's a good thing you didn't go with them!"

Turn to page 51.

Soon you settle into a routine, getting up early with Ruth every day and going to work in Boaz's field. After a few days, your muscles no longer ache, and the hospitality shown by Boaz makes it a pleasure to go to work. Before you even realize it, it's almost the end of the harvest. Then one night Naomi comes to Ruth with some important news.

"I've heard that Boaz will winnow his barley harvest tonight at the threshing floor," she says. She explains that winnowing is the separation of the grains of barley from the small pieces of straw, which were mixed in from the field. This is done by throwing both the grains and the straw into the air so that the wind blows away the straw, which is lighter.

"Ruth, my daughter," she continues, "you must bathe, put on perfume and your best clothes and go to where Boaz is working tonight. Don't let him know you're there until he has finished eating and drinking after the winnowing. Then, when he lies down to rest, lie at his feet, and he will tell you what to do." (It was the Jewish custom at that time for the closest male relative to marry and take care of the widow of a deceased family member. Naomi is sending Ruth to Boaz hoping that Ruth will ask him to marry her.)

"I'll do just as you say," Ruth answers Naomi.

You follow Ruth as she goes to get her best robe. "Would you like me to come with you tonight?" you ask her.

"It's up to you," she replies with a smile. "I'd like you to come, but it might be best to stay here so that Naomi won't be alone."

If you go to the threshing floor with Ruth, turn to page 54.

If you stay with Naomi, turn to page 57.

"I'll come with you," you tell Ruth. "Naomi will be fine for one night. I want to be there, just in case you need me."

Ruth thanks you, and you both get ready. At sundown you excitedly set out. You wonder what Boaz will tell Ruth.

Approaching his field, you see a large pile of barley, the result of the threshing just completed. At one end of the pile is a table, well lit by the hanging lamps that surround it. Boaz is at the head of the table, happily enjoying the celebration with his workers. You see that the long table is piled high with food and drink of every kind.

"I must wait," Ruth whispers, "until Boaz finishes and lies down."

You and Ruth find a spot on a small nearby hill and sit down to wait. You have a good view of the field below. The party continues, as Boaz toasts his workers and leads them in a joyous song thanking the Lord for the harvest. After a few more songs, Boaz stands up and yawns, then walks away from the table to the far end of the pile of barley.

"I'll go to him now," Ruth says quietly.

"Would you like me to stay and keep watch, just in case you need me?" you ask her.

"Yes, thank you," Ruth replies. "That would make me feel better. But you probably don't need to remain the whole night. When all is well, I'll wave to you and you can go back to stay with Naomi."

Ruth smiles and quickly climbs down the hill. When she reaches the road, some workers are already leaving the feast. Ruth greets them, then continues on toward Boaz. The workers are laughing and singing. One of them suddenly notices you watching from the hill.

"Friend!" he shouts. "Why are you sitting alone while everyone else is celebrating the harvest?"

You explain what you're doing, and the workers laugh.

"Your friend is very safe if she's with Boaz," one man says. "We remember how hard you worked in the fields. Come, continue the celebration with us in the city."

You're very happy that the workers are so friendly and feel flattered that they've invited you to celebrate with them. You see that Ruth is almost to the spot where Boaz is lying down, and you wonder if the workers are right about her safety. On the other hand, you did make a promise to Ruth.

If you go with the workers to celebrate in the city, turn to page 58.

If you stay and keep watch for Ruth, turn to page 59.

"It's probably best that you go alone, Ruth," you reply.

She nods in agreement.

Soon it's evening, and Ruth sets off for Boaz's field. As soon as the door closes, Naomi leads you in a prayer for her.

You spend a quiet evening with Naomi. She tells you wonderful stories of her life, and of her personal relationship with God. This, she explains, is why she isn't worried about Ruth tonight.

"The Lord will provide for us," she whispers.

You go to bed early and sleep very peacefully. At a certain point, you're awakened by a gentle touch on your shoulder. You open your eyes to find Ruth standing over you, smiling.

Turn to page 60.

You reason that Ruth will probably be safe with Boaz, and you see that she's almost reached the field as you set off down the hill and join the workers. They warmly welcome you and soon you're all marching down the road singing songs of praise to the God of Israel.

As you enter Bethlehem's gates, your voices echo from the city walls. People open doors and look out windows as you pass, many of them cheering their encouragement. After winding through the streets, you reach a small square, where the celebration continues with more food and drink.

You're having a wonderful time, but soon you begin to think about Ruth. You wonder if she's alright, and you feel guilty about having broken your promise to her. You decide to return to Boaz's field in order to check on her. It's very dark now, and once you've left the lights of the city behind, it's difficult to find your way. You finally come to a crossroad. But which is the road that will bring you back to Ruth? You have no idea….

The End

"Thank you for your invitation, but I must keep my promise to my friend," you explain. The workers wish you well and set off toward the city, breaking into another happy song as they go.

Now you turn your attention back to Ruth. You see that she's reached the spot where Boaz lies sleeping, and you watch as she takes her place at his feet, as Naomi instructed her to. She gently pulls back the blanket covering his feet and lies down. After a few minutes, she waves in your direction, and you know that everything is all right.

You stay and watch for a few minutes, just to be sure, then leave for the city. You easily find your way back to Naomi's house. She's waiting for you and is very happy to hear of Ruth's safe passage to Boaz.

You end a long day by going to bed and quickly falling asleep.

The next morning you're awakened by the sound of soft footsteps, and you sit up to find Ruth sitting at the table.

Turn to page 60.

"Good morning, my friends," Ruth cheerfully greets you and Naomi.

"Tell us what happened," Naomi eagerly says, resting her hand on Ruth's shoulder.

Ruth tells how Boaz woke up during the night. Surprised to find her at his feet, he asked who she was. She told him that she was a relative of his, and she asked him to take her under his care by marrying her. Boaz was very happy. He told Ruth that the Lord would bless her because she had always been kind and good. He told her that all the townspeople considered her a virtuous woman. "I would gladly marry you," Boaz explained to Ruth, "but you do have one other closer relative. He has the first right and duty to buy the property that belonged to Naomi's husband and marry you. I will speak with this man. If he doesn't wish to buy the land and marry you, as the Lord lives, I will." Boaz then told Ruth that she could sleep there at his threshing floor for the rest of the night. Early the next morning he filled her veil with barley from his harvest. He didn't want her to go back to Naomi empty-handed.

"This is so wonderful!" cries Naomi. "Boaz is a good man. Now you must wait here, for he'll certainly take care of things today."

The three of you enjoy a celebration breakfast. Then Naomi asks you to go out and buy some leaven so she can bake bread. Leaven is an important ingredient in the process, since it's used to make the bread dough rise. Eager to help, you set out for the market.

On your way to the market square, you hear someone calling your name. You turn around to find one of Boaz's chief servants, who says he's on his way to meet Boaz at the city gate. He explains that the gate is where people gather to take care of various business matters. "Boaz is going there now to speak with Naomi's closest relative about buying Elimelech's land and marrying Ruth. He'll have the elders act as his witnesses," the servant informs you. "This is wonderful news for your friend Ruth. Maybe you'd like to come with me and watch."

You think of how exciting it would be to see Boaz speaking of Ruth in front of the city elders, but you don't want to keep Naomi waiting.

If you go watch Boaz before the elders, turn to page 62.

If you get the leaven and return to Naomi and Ruth, turn to page 67.

"I'd love to come with you!" you tell Boaz's servant, thinking that the leaven can wait.

"Good! This way," he says, as he leads you off through the twisting streets.

After a brisk walk you arrive at the main gate to the city, where a bustling crowd of people is gathered beneath the bright morning sun. In a few minutes the crowd parts and you see Boaz, wearing a very beautiful robe, arrive. He takes a seat on a bench near the gate and calls out in a loud voice to a man standing nearby. The man approaches. Next Boaz asks that the elders come forward. Slowly ten older men come out of the crowd and take their seats on surrounding benches.

"You're a closer relative to Naomi than am I," Boaz says, addressing the man. "She's selling a parcel of land which belonged to her husband Elimelech, and you're first in line to buy it."

"I will buy it," the man says.

"Know then," Boaz adds, "that with the field you buy not only the land of Naomi, but also the hand of her daughter-in-law, Ruth."

"Then I'm unable to buy it," says the man, "for I would not be able to provide for them both. I give this right to you."

The man then takes off his sandal and hands it to Boaz. The servant sees the puzzled look on

your face and whispers that the passing of a sandal is the traditional way of making an agreement official.

"Then let all present be witnesses that on this day I buy Elimelech's land," Boaz says loudly, "and with it the hand in marriage of Ruth the Moabite."

One of the elders stands and addresses Boaz. "We are witnesses. The Lord shall let Ruth become your wife, and we wish you nothing but happiness."

The crowd breaks into a cheer and people come forward to congratulate Boaz. As you're awaiting your turn, you overhear a couple in front of you talking.

"His bride-to-be is from our homeland," says the woman to her husband.

"Excuse me," you break in. "I couldn't help hearing you. I'm also from Moab."

"We've come to Bethlehem to trade some of our goods," the husband explains. "We'll be returning to Moab later today."

The woman notices the homesick look on your face. "You're welcome to join us on our journey back," she kindly tells you.

By now you've made your way up to Boaz. The husband and wife congratulate him and step aside.

Boaz immediately recognizes you and greets you with a big smile.

"I hope to see you at our wedding," he says.

If you tell him that you've decided to return to Moab, turn to page 66.

If you tell him that you'll be there at the wedding, turn to page 68.

"I'm sorry," you apologize to Boaz. "I'd love to come to the wedding, but I've just been given the opportunity to return to Moab, my homeland, and I feel that I should go."

"I know how Ruth will miss you, but you must follow your heart," Boaz answers quietly. "I wish you health and blessings."

You thank Boaz for all his kindness and turn back to find the Moabite couple.

Turn to page 32.

"I appreciate the invitation," you tell the servant, "but I need to get back to Naomi and Ruth."

"As you wish," he says. "Please excuse me now. I don't want to be late."

He heads off through the crowd, and you continue in the opposite direction to the marketplace. You're so anxious to return to the house that it seems like forever before you're waited on. Finally a merchant hands you the leaven. You pay for it and rush back to Naomi's.

Turn to page 69.

"Of course I'll be there!" you exclaim. "I wouldn't miss it for the world!"

"Marvelous," Boaz replies.

You say good-bye to Boaz, then turn and thank the Moabite couple for their offer, wishing them a safe journey. As you start back to Naomi's, you suddenly remember your unfinished errand. Quickly continuing on to the market, you purchase the leaven, then hurry back to Naomi and Ruth.

Turn to page 69.

Turning down the street where Naomi lives, you see that a small crowd has gathered outside her house. You reach the front just in time to see Ruth coming out with Boaz. A ripple of approval runs through the crowd. *They must have announced their wedding plans,* you think.

You've never seen your friend Ruth look so happy. Standing back while neighbors and friends surround the couple, you approach when everyone else has left. Ruth greets you with a hug that almost takes your breath away. "How happy I am that your God has blessed you!" you whisper in her ear.

"Yes, it's true," she says. "I trusted him, and he provided for me."

You turn to Naomi and hand her the leaven. She breaks into a big smile and the two of you laugh out loud.

"The bread can wait," she says. "We have a wedding to plan!"

The following weeks are a blur of activity. There are so many preparations to make. In the time between the engagement and the wedding Boaz is not allowed to see Ruth, so you act as the messenger between the two of them, also delivering the many gifts Boaz sends Ruth.

Finally the great day arrives. The ceremony begins toward evening. You and Naomi wear beautiful robes prepared for you by Boaz. Ruth looks lovely in her flowing, gold-embroidered robe and gorgeous jewelry. Boaz heads a procession of singers and musicians to Naomi's house. Upon their arrival, Naomi leads Ruth, covered with a veil, to Boaz. Now the procession winds its way back through the city to Boaz's house, where the short wedding ceremony takes place. A magnificent feast follows. The celebration features musicians, dancers, joke-tellers, and many other kinds of entertainment. It goes on for days.

After the excitement of the wedding there is a welcome calm as life settles back to normal. You spend most of your time helping Naomi. You still see Ruth of course, but not as often as before her marriage. Soon comes the good news that the Lord has blessed Ruth and Boaz with a child. You're happy to be there when the beautiful, healthy little boy is born. A few days later, Ruth calls you into her chamber.

"My dear friend," she says, "Naomi will be taking care of my child, and I know that you would be a great help to her. At the same time, I could use your help in managing our large household. Would you be willing to take on one of these du-

ties? Either way, we'll still be close and we'll see each other very often."

If you decide to help Naomi take care of the baby, turn to page 73.

If you'd like to help Ruth run her household, turn to page 74.

"I'd love to help Naomi care for your child," you tell Ruth.

"Thank you," she says. "I know my son is in good hands."

You enjoy looking after Ruth's baby. Every day women from throughout the city come to visit Naomi and see the child. They talk of how the Lord has blessed Naomi in making sure she is not left without a kinsman. The women name the child Obed, proclaiming that his name will become famous in Israel.

You live out your life in Bethlehem, helping Naomi raise Obed. You see Ruth often and make many other wonderful friends as well. Though you still think of your homeland sometimes, you're so happy in Bethlehem, and your heart is so full of the Lord's peace, that Moab seems like another world to you.

Obed grows up to be a fine young man. It turns out that the neighbor women were right: Obed one day has a son named Jesse, and Jesse then has a son named David, who becomes the King of Israel. But that's another story...

The End

"Both choices are wonderful," you tell Ruth, "but since I can only have one, I'd like to stay at your house as your personal assistant."

Ruth smiles and embraces you warmly.

"You've been such a good friend throughout the years," she says. "I look forward to many more years of friendship."

You do spend many more happy years with your friend Ruth. In your work for Ruth and Boaz you develop a reputation for dependability and industriousness. Boaz rewards you by making you an overseer at the harvest. The Lord also rewards you by allowing you to meet a kind and loving man among the harvesters. Although you get married and have a family of your own, you continue to live just outside of Bethlehem and always remain close to your best friend Ruth.

The End

Multiple-Ending Bible Adventures

At the Side of David

At the Side of Esther

At the Side of Moses

At the Side of Ruth

BOOKS & MEDIA

The Daughters of St. Paul operate book and media centers at the following addresses. Visit, call or write the one nearest you today, or find us on the World Wide Web, www.pauline.org

California
3908 Sepulveda Blvd., Culver City, CA 90230; 310-397-8676
5945 Balboa Ave., San Diego, CA 92111; 858-565-9181
46 Geary Street, San Francisco, CA 94108; 415-781-5180

Florida
145 S.W. 107th Ave., Miami, FL 33174; 305-559-6715

Hawaii
1143 Bishop Street, Honolulu, HI 96813; 808-521-2731

Neighbor Islands call: 800-259-8463

Illinois
172 North Michigan Ave., Chicago, IL 60601; 312-346-4228

Louisiana
4403 Veterans Memorial Blvd., Metairie, LA 70006; 504-887-7631

Massachusetts
Rte. 1, 885 Providence Hwy., Dedham, MA 02026; 781-326-5385

Missouri
9804 Watson Rd., St. Louis, MO 63126; 314-965-3512

New Jersey
561 U.S. Route 1, Wick Plaza, Edison, NJ 08817; 732-572-1200

New York
150 East 52nd Street, New York, NY 10022; 212-754-1110
78 Fort Place, Staten Island, NY 10301; 718-447-5071

Ohio
2105 Ontario Street, Cleveland, OH 44115; 216-621-9427

Pennsylvania
9171-A Roosevelt Blvd., Philadelphia, PA 19114; 215-676-9494

South Carolina
243 King Street, Charleston, SC 29401; 843-577-0175

Tennessee
4811 Poplar Ave., Memphis, TN 38117; 901-761-2987

Texas
114 Main Plaza, San Antonio, TX 78205; 210-224-8101

Virginia
1025 King Street, Alexandria, VA 22314; 703-549-3806

Canada
3022 Dufferin Street, Toronto, Ontario, Canada M6B 3T5; 416-781-9131
1155 Yonge Street, Toronto, Ontario, Canada M4T 1W2; 416-934-3440

¡También somos su fuente para libros, videos y música en español!